TOMMY O'TOM IN
A TUB O'TROUBLE

JTK BELLE & MIKE MOTZ

Picklefish
Press

Printed in the United States of America
Third Printing, 2018

Hardcover ISBN: 978-0-692-05463-5
Paperback ISBN: 978-1-976-89162-5

JTK Belle is Jeff, Tommy, and Katie Belle.
Editor: Katie Belle
Creative Director: Tommy Belle
Illustrations by Mike Motz
Book Design by Michelle M White

Picklefish Press
www.picklefishpress.com

For Milo
and
Penny

Tommy O'Tom

was taking a bath

2

when in walked a **hippo** — and then a giraffe.

3

To Tommy's surprise,
they climbed over
the side

4

and jumped into the tub with a **splash!**

"Boy are we dirty,"
they said.
They wrapped towels
around on their heads.

6

"Tommy O'Tom!
Hurry up!" called his mom
"It's time to get ready for bed!"

7

They splashed **water**
all over the floor.
They got mud on the rug
and the door.

8

A **flamingo** came in with a shake of his wings

10

and said, **"Do you have room for one more?"**

11

Said Hippo, "We certainly do – and for Zebra and Elephant too!"

"Can you pass me the scrubber?
Hey, this duck's made of rubber!
This sure beats the pond at the zoo!"

The giraffe wrote Tommy's name on the mirror.
The elephant cleaned out his ears.

"Tommy O' Tom!
Hurry up!" called his mom.
"It's bedtime already, my dear!"

15

There were feathers all over the place.

On Tommy's shoulders.
And his back.
And his **face.**

Then Hippo got out and **blew out his snout**

and said **"There's just not enough space."**

19

"And this water's too cold," he complained.
"We might as well stand in the rain."
He said "Let's make it hotter!"

and turned on the **water** and pulled out the plug from the **drain**.

Then Elephant turned on the **shower** —
and watered the wallpaper flowers.

22

"Tommy O'Tom! Hurry up!" called his mom.
"You've been in there for nearly an hour!"

23

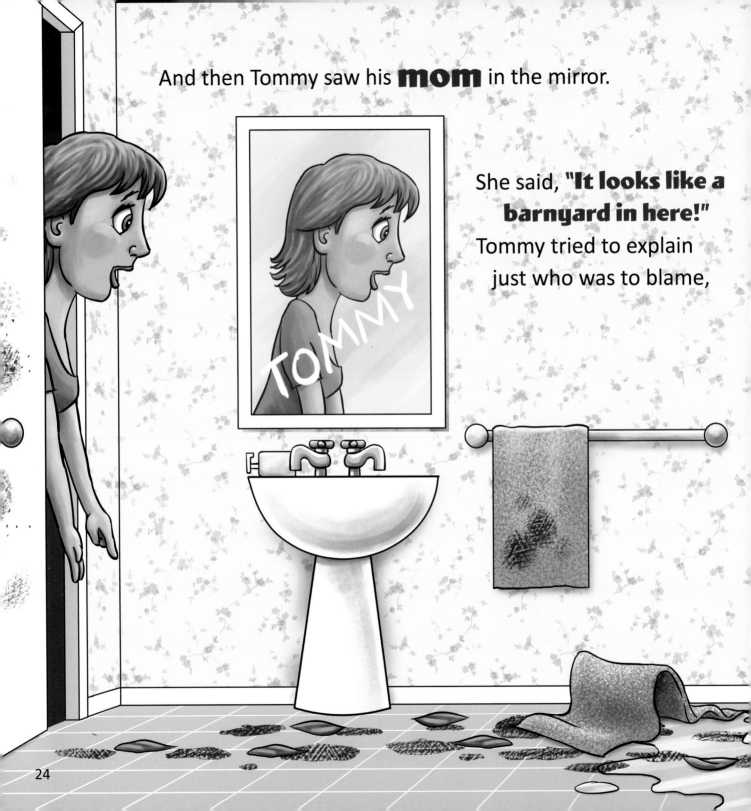

And then Tommy saw his **mom** in the mirror.

She said, **"It looks like a barnyard in here!"**
Tommy tried to explain just who was to blame,

TOMMY

but the animals had all **disappeared!**

JTK Belle

is Jeff, Tommy, and Katie Belle.
They live in Seattle, Washington.

Also by JTK Belle:

Katherine's Bike was Wonderfully Strange

Kids love their bikes, and what child hasn't imagined their bike could fly? Whenever Katherine rides her magical new bike, high adventure awaits. With each shift of the gears comes a change in the weather, as Katherine goes exploring — from the streets of her neighborhood to the starry skies above.

Beautifully-illustrated, with a whimsical, rhyming text, Katherine's Bike Was Wonderfully Strange is a perfect read-aloud for the end of the day.

FREEDA THE CHEETAH

Kids love animals, and what child doesn't love a good game of hide-and-go-seek? But who is the world's very best player of hide-and-go-seek? Why, Freed the Cheetah, of course. Freeda the Cheetah of Mozambique.

As the elephant covers his eyes with his trunk and counts to a hundred, the animals of the savanna scatter in every direction. Elephant finds every one of them, from the hippo in the muddy water to the monkeys behind the bananas. But he just can't find that unfindable cheetah. Soon all the other animals join in on the search — even the lion and the blue wildebeests — as the colors of the savanna begin to fade into the evening. Will they find her before bedtime?

Connect with JTK Belle

 www.facebook.com/PicklefishPress

 www.twitter.com/jtkbelle

 www.picklefishpress.com